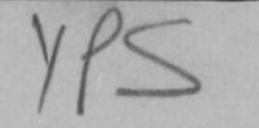
YPS

D0996394

# Usborne Stories from Around the World for Little Children

# Contents

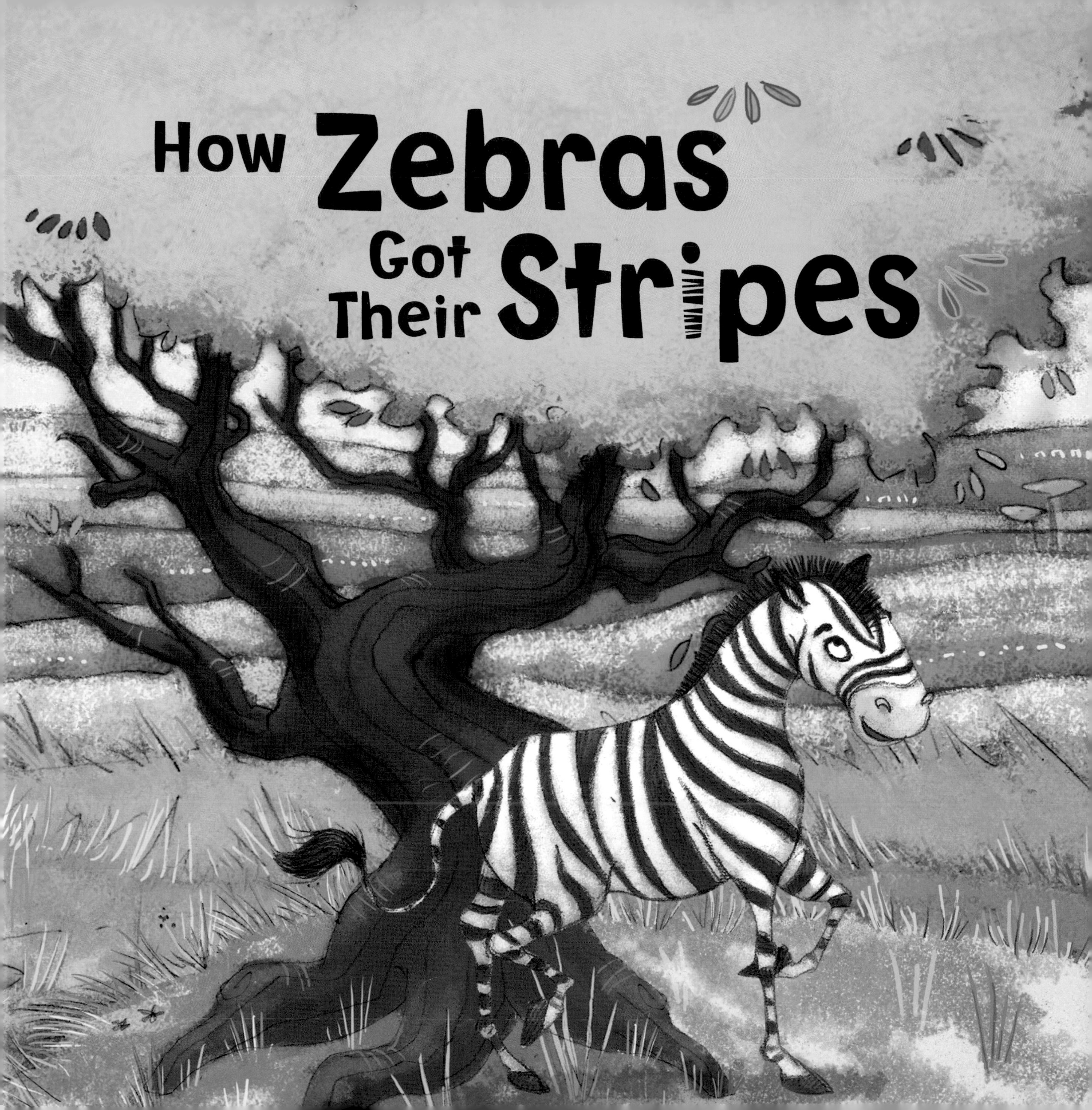
How Zebras Got Their Stripes

Once upon a time, on a dusty African plain, there lived...

a greedy baboon...

a gentle giraffe...

an amiable elephant...

and the world's
very first zebra.

The greedy baboon lived
by the side of a pond.

He thought the pond
belonged to him.

He sploshed and he splashed, from dawn until dusk, playing in the water.

One summer, it was so hot, the sun scorched the clouds from the sky.

Everyone was desperately thirsty.

Baboon didn't care a bit.

Giraffe was longing for just one sip of clear, cool water.

She crept up to the pond and...

...Baboon leaped out from behind a tree.
“Go away you galumphing giraffe!” he shouted.
“Find your own pond!”

Giraffe turned tail and fled.

Elephant imagined sucking the water up into his trunk. It would slip down his dry throat, soothing and refreshing. So he, too, crept up to the pond.

Now Baboon was angry.
"Go away you enraging elephant!" he screamed.
"Find your own pond!"

The ground shook as Elephant ran away.

Zebra had seen Baboon being mean.
He trotted over to the pond.

Baboon was jumping up and down in a frenzy of rage.

Zebra simply snorted and stamped his hoof.

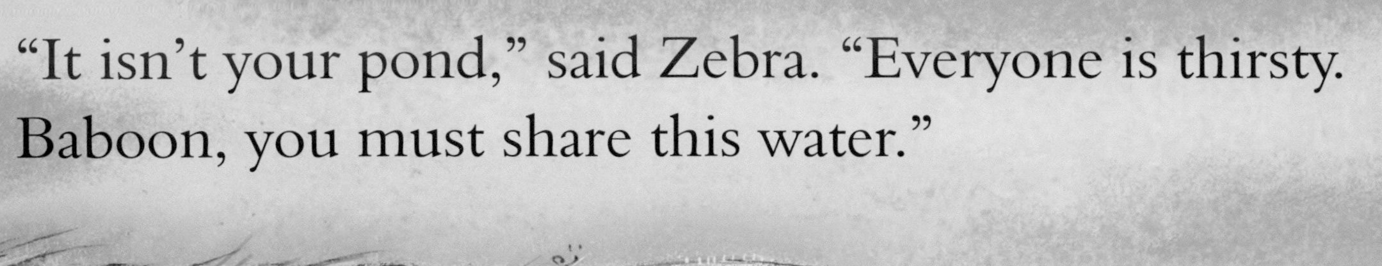

"It isn't your pond," said Zebra. "Everyone is thirsty. Baboon, you must share this water."

"No!" said Baboon. "I don't want to. Go away and leave me alone."

Baboon turned his back on Zebra.

He began to collect armfuls of sticks.

Then he piled them into a pyramid by the pond.

He made some sparks and set fire to the sticks.
Flames crackled and smoke
billowed into the air.

"Ha!" he said. "That
should keep everyone
away - even Zebra."

But Zebra wasn't scared.
He was extremely annoyed.

He gave the fiercest
snort he could...

...and galloped over to where Baboon sat by the fire.

Without stopping, he struck Baboon with his front legs.

Baboon went flying
into the air...

...and so did the
sooty sticks from his fire.

The sticks scattered back down and bounced off Zebra, leaving sooty black stripes all over his body.

Baboon landed with a **THUMP!** on his bottom.

And that is why, to this very day, all zebras have black stripes...

...and baboons have red bottoms.

# Brer Rabbit Down the Well

Brer Rabbit and Brer Fox were sworn enemies.

Brer Rabbit was always hiding from Brer Fox, who was always trying to catch him.

“Where are you,
rascal rabbit?”
called Brer Fox.

Brer Rabbit shot out from behind his tree and headed for a field.

Brer Fox chased after him.

“I’m going to eat you up, wretched rabbit,” snarled Brer Fox.

Brer Rabbit laughed. “You’ll never catch me!”

Puffing and panting, he reached a well.

It was so deep, he couldn't see the bottom.

But he could see a bucket. "That would be the perfect place to hide," he thought.

So he jumped into the bucket.

The handle rattled
and spun...

the rope loosened
and the bucket plummeted into the well.

The bucket fell down...

and down...

and down...

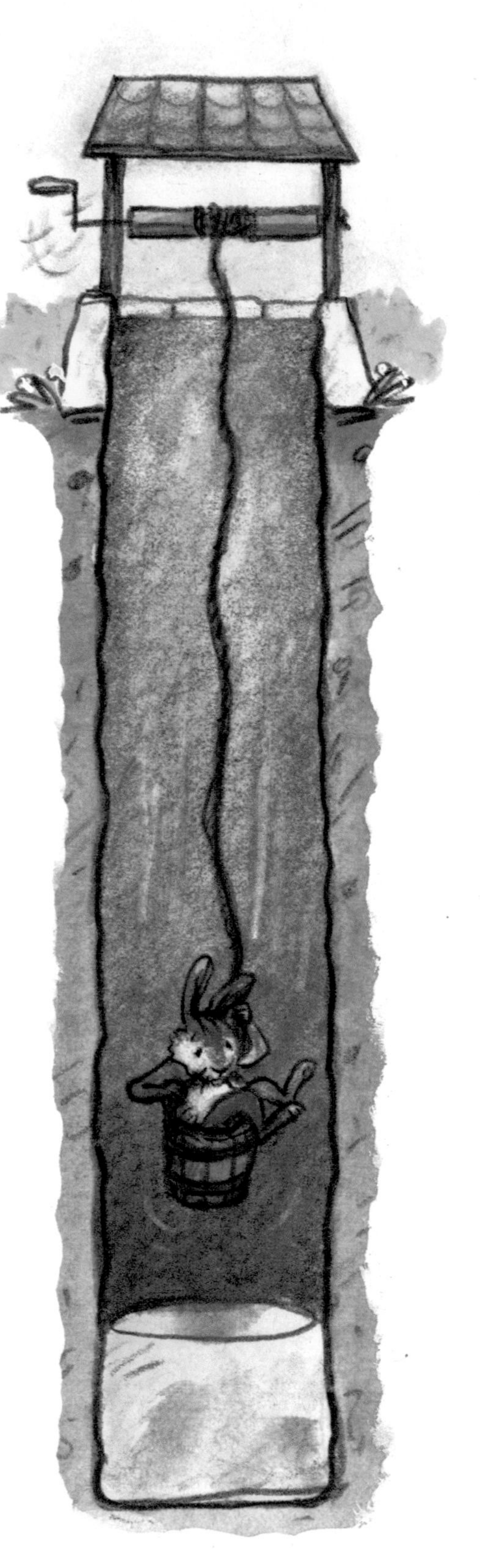

...until it landed with
a colossal splash.

"Uh-oh," thought Brer Rabbit.
"How will I ever get out?"

"Ha! Ha!" cried a gleeful voice. "Found you!"

Brer Rabbit looked up.

There, grinning back at him,
was the smug face of Brer Fox.

"You can't hide from me!"
Brer Fox growled.

“Oh, I’m not hiding,” said Brer Rabbit.
“Why would you think that?”

“I’m fishing!”

"There are some splendid fish down here. I've never seen such huge trout."

He plunged his paw into the water and splashed it around.

"Hurray! I've caught one,"
cried Brer Rabbit.
"And it's a beauty."

"Ooh! And there's another!"

"You should come down here,"
he added. "Or there won't be any left."

Now, Brer Fox loved fish. The thought of eating freshly grilled trout made his snout twitch and his mouth water.

He forgot all about catching Brer Rabbit.

Quickly, he turned the well handle.
Rattling and creaking, the bucket rose up.

As soon as the bucket reached the top,
Brer Rabbit jumped out and Brer Fox climbed in.

The handle rattled and spun...

the rope loosened...

and the bucket
plummeted
into the well.

Down...

down...

down...

Finally, it hit the
water with a splash.

Brer Rabbit looked into the deep, dark well.
He grinned at Brer Fox.

Then he began to laugh.

"Where are the fish?" shouted Brer Fox.
"I can't see any here at all."

"The fish are in the river of course," said Brer Rabbit, still chuckling. "In fact, I think I'll go and catch some right now."

Brer Fox howled with rage. "You rotten, rascal rabbit. You tricked me!"

But Brer Rabbit had
already strolled away.

Brer Fox did manage to climb out of the well in the end... but it took him all night.

# The Dragon Painter

Chang's
House

Chang was a painter. Everyone loved his pictures. People came from all over China to see them.

Chang painted misty mountains
with craggy rocks and
tumbling waterfalls.

He painted pots filled
with beautiful blossoms.

But his animal pictures were best of all. His butterflies seemed to flutter on the paper.

His birds had a lively twinkle in their eyes – and you could almost see his rabbits twitch their noses.

Chang and his pictures became famous.

Even the Emperor of China heard about them.

"Summon Chang to the palace!" he ordered. "I need a painter to decorate my new temple."

Chang bowed low before the Emperor. "I will do my best for you," he promised.

Chang planned a splendid display. "I'll paint four dragons," he thought. "One on each wall."

Large crowds gathered to watch Chang paint.

On the first wall, he painted a dragon with scales of shimmering pearl.

Clouds of steam billowed from its mouth.

Only one thing was missing.

The dragon had no eyes.

A jade-green dragon leaped out from the second wall.

It had bushy eyebrows and
a sharp, spiked nose.

But this dragon's eyes
were missing too.

The third dragon was shining gold, with a long, coiled tail, curling around its body.

The gold dragon didn't have any eyes either.

"Why aren't you painting their eyes?" asked the people watching him. Chang simply smiled and kept on painting.

The last dragon was the most magnificent of all.

It had fiery-red scales...

wicked claws...

and snapping jaws...

...but it still had no eyes.

Chang put down his paintbrush and turned to the Emperor. "Do you like my dragons, sire?" he asked.

"Very much," said the Emperor. "But where are their eyes?"

"Oh, I can't paint their eyes, sire," said Chang. "Dragons are magical creatures. If I paint their eyes, they will come to life!"

“Nonsense!” said the Emperor. “I won’t have unfinished dragons on my walls. Paint in their eyes this minute!”

Chang had no choice but to obey the Emperor. With a wobbly hand, he painted in the eyes of the pearl-white dragon.

BOOM!

A rumble of thunder shook the temple.

The sky grew dark.

Chang paused.

"What are you waiting for?" boomed the Emperor, almost as loud as the thunder. "Get on with it!"

So Chang dotted in the eyes
of the jade dragon...

...the gold dragon...

...and the fearsome,
fiery-red dragon.

As Chang finished...
CRACK!
...a bolt of lightning slammed into the temple roof and burst it open.

The jade dragon blinked once... twice... and lifted its head.

Its spiky nose cracked one of the temple columns.

The pearl dragon yawned, showing its sharp, white teeth. It breathed out clouds of burning steam.

The people nearby ran for their lives.

With a roar, both dragons jumped from their walls.

They soared into the air and flew through the hole in the roof.

They rose higher and higher, until they disappeared altogether.

Chang saw the red and gold dragons begin to stir. He snatched up his brush and painted strong chains around their necks.

However much they rattled their chains,
the dragons couldn't fly away.

The Emperor had to be content with only two dragons on the walls of his temple.

But everyone agreed they were the best painted dragons in all of China.

# Why the Sea is Salty

Long, long ago, the world was very different.
Even the sea wasn't salty, but sweet and good to drink.

So why, you might wonder, is the sea not sweet today? Well, it all began with a magic millstone.

The millstone belonged to a mighty king.

Most millstones are used
to make flour, but
this millstone...

...made piles of gold and
sparkling jewels.

It made tempting treats
and special spices...

...or whatever the king
asked for.

One day, a thief met a friend who told him all about the magic millstone.

"I want it!" thought the thief.

"I'll be richer than I've ever dreamed."

He scratched his head. "I just have to find out where the king keeps it."

So he went
to the palace.

A friendly guard gave the thief a grand tour.

He saw the gardens...

...and the throne room, but he couldn't see the magic millstone anywhere.

In the royal bedroom, he had an idea.

"This palace is magnificent," he said to the guard. "But I'm sorry not to see the magic millstone. I expect the king keeps it hidden?"

The guard laughed. "Of course he does," he replied. "It is his greatest treasure, after all."

As they walked, the thief kept chatting.

“I bet you don’t even know where the millstone is kept,” he teased the guard.

“Oh yes I do,” said the guard. “Under the king’s bed.”

"What a clever hiding place," said the thief.

"And I suppose you have to be a great magician to make the millstone work."

"Oh no," said the guard. "The king simply taps it three times and asks for what he wants."

Later that night, the thief crept back to the palace.

He tiptoed into the king's bedroom, lifted the mattress...

...and grabbed the millstone.

Hiding the millstone under his cloak,
he raced away as fast as he could.

He ran all the way to the sea, where he leaped into a waiting boat and sailed away.

Out at sea, the thief gazed at the millstone. “I can have anything I want!” he thought. “What shall I ask for first?”

He took out a bun to nibble
while he decided.
The bun didn't taste too good.
"Pah!" he spat. "That needs salt."

So he tapped the millstone
three times and asked in a clear
voice, "Please may I have
some salt?"

At once, the millstone began turning
and bright white salt poured out.

The thief fell asleep
with a smile on his face,
dreaming of riches.

All night long, the magical
millstone kept turning.

The pile of salt
grew bigger...

...and bigger...

...and bigger.

Still the millstone kept turning.
The thief woke up to a mountain of salt towering over him.

"Stop now!" shouted the thief, but the millstone didn't stop. "That's enough!" he yelled, but the millstone kept on turning. The mountain of salt piled higher.

The salt was so heavy that the boat began to sink in the water.

Before long, waves were slopping over the sides – and still the millstone kept turning...

Frantically, the thief burrowed into the salt.

"I have to stop that millstone," he gasped. But it was buried far too deep.

The millstone kept on turning until, finally, the boat sank.

The magic millstone went with it, sinking down to the bottom of the ocean.

The thief swam home, where
an angry king stood on the shore,
waiting for him.

As for the millstone – it is
still at the bottom of the sea,
pouring out salt to this very day.

# Aladdin
## & His Magical Lamp

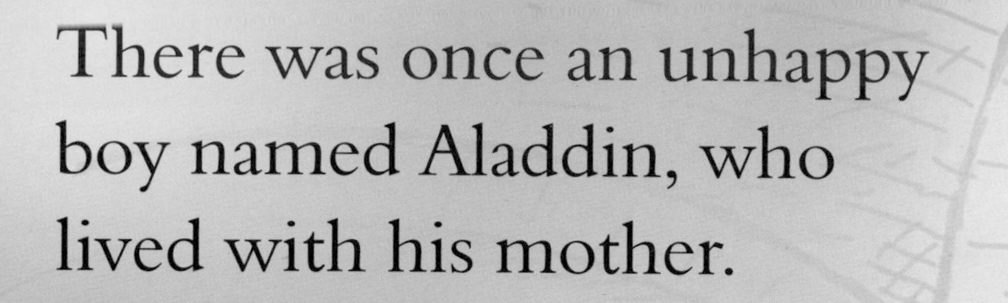

There was once an unhappy boy named Aladdin, who lived with his mother.

He spent most days dreaming they were rich.

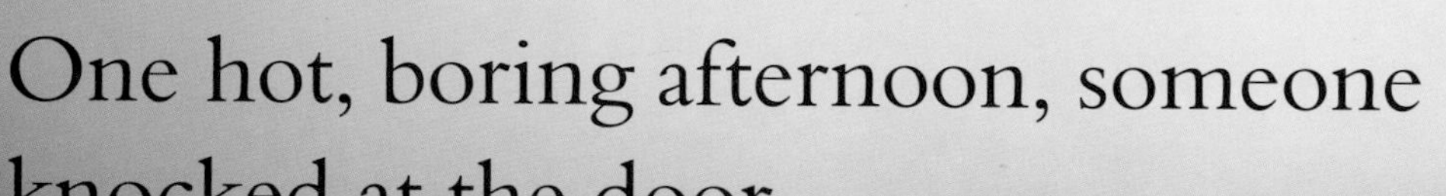

One hot, boring afternoon, someone knocked at the door.

Aladdin opened the door to see a complete stranger.

"Are you Aladdin?" said the man. "I'm your long-lost uncle, Abanazar."

"I've brought you a gift," he added, handing Aladdin a ring. "But in return I need your help."

"I'll do what I can," said Aladdin, following Abanazar to a quiet spot out of town.

Abanazar stopped, waved his hands and...

KAZAM!

...a trap door appeared in the ground.

"Wow!" said Aladdin.

To his surprise, his uncle opened the door and shoved him through. "There's a lamp down there," he said. "Find it!"

Aladdin stumbled into a cavern. Ahead of him were strange trees, growing fruit that glowed in the darkness. He paused to pick some.

Then he spotted the lamp shining in a corner and popped it in his pocket.

“Look at this!” Aladdin called out, showing Abanazar an armful of the fruit.

“You silly boy, I said find the lamp!” snapped his uncle, and he slammed the trap door shut with a bang.

"Help!" Aladdin shouted. "Uncle? Don't leave me." He shivered and rubbed his hands and...

PING!

...a genie appeared.

"Behold! I am the genie of the ring," he said. "What is your wish?"

"I just want to go home," Aladdin wailed.

"Done!" said the genie.

Back home,
Aladdin's mother
looked at the lamp.

"We can sell this," she said, rubbing off a speck of dust.
A fountain of stars sprayed
into the air and...

WHOOSH!

...an enormous genie
floated out.

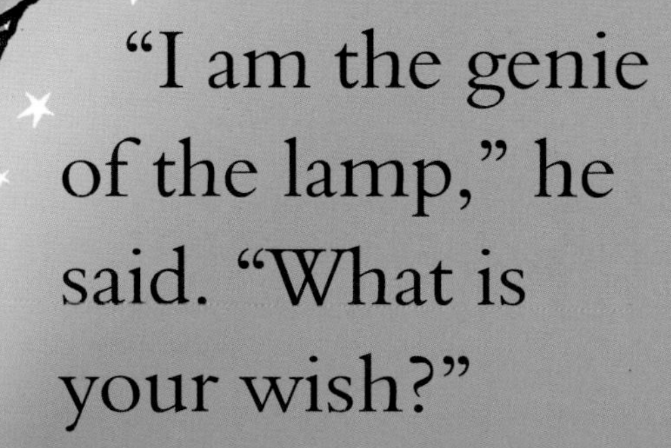

"I am the genie
of the lamp," he
said. "What is
your wish?"

Goodness me!

Aladdin's mother was shocked but she thought quickly. "Jewels!" she cried – and Aladdin's hands filled with giant sapphires, emeralds, pearls and rubies. At last, he was rich.

Several days later, Aladdin was passing the palace when he saw the Sultan's only daughter, Princess Badra.

As he gazed at her face, he fell in love.

"Now I'm rich, I can marry!" he told his mother. "And it has to be Princess Badra. She's the only girl for me."

"Mother, will you take our jewels as a gift to the Sultan and ask him if she can be my wife?"

"What splendid gems!"
said the Sultan, when he saw
the jewels. "Do you have more?"

Hearing this, Aladdin went straight to the lamp and summoned the genie.

WHOOSH!

"What is your wish?" asked the genie.

"Fill the Sultan's palace with jewels," Aladdin commanded.

"Done!" said the genie,
with a grin.

The Sultan was delighted.

"Your son shall marry Princess Badra tomorrow!" he declared.

Aladdin had just one more request.

"I'd like Princess Badra to live in style," he told the genie. "Could you build a palace? I have a list of what I want in each room."

The royal wedding was held the very next day.

One thousand guests feasted, danced and cheered in delight as Aladdin married his princess.

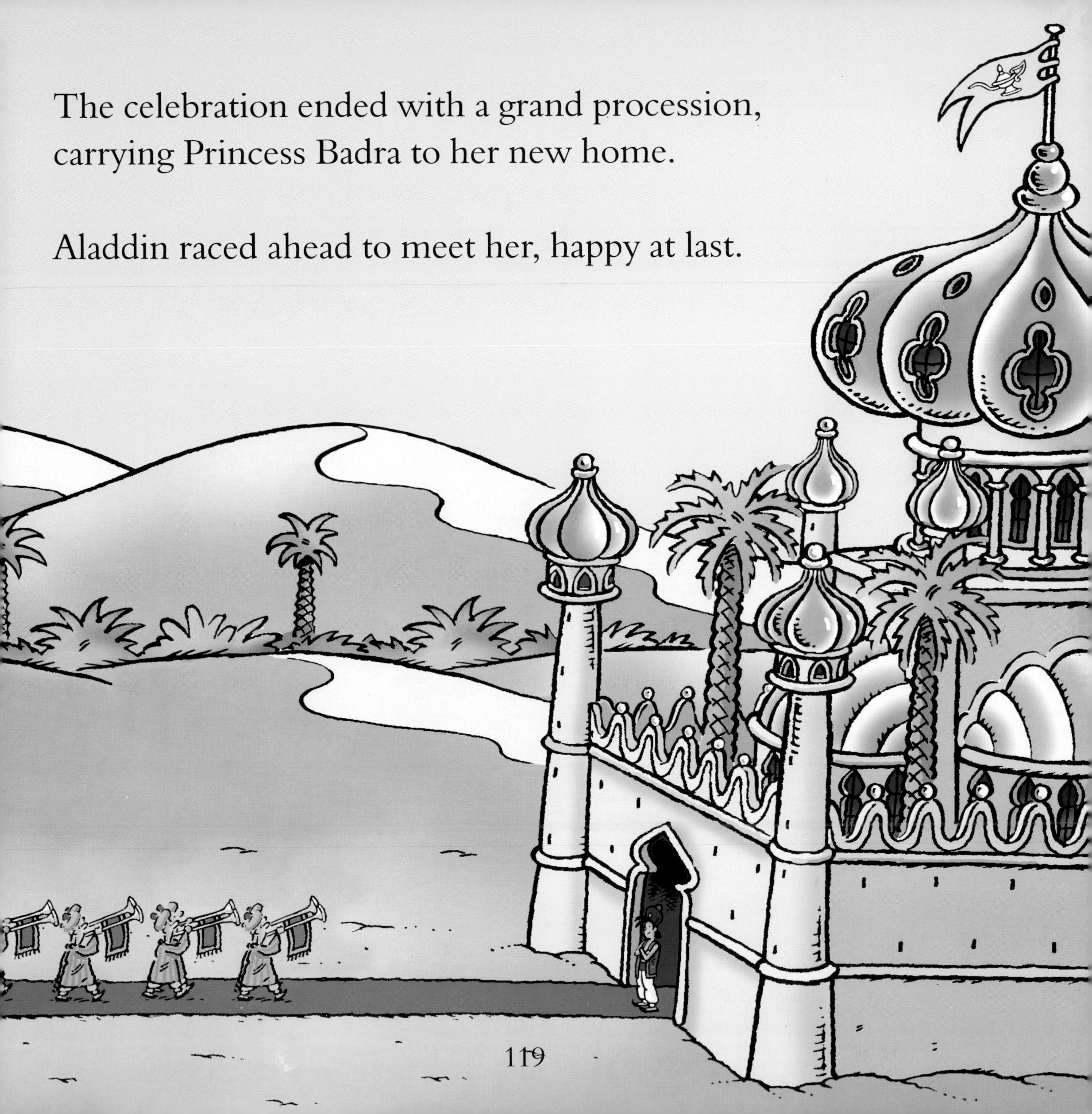

The celebration ended with a grand procession, carrying Princess Badra to her new home.

Aladdin raced ahead to meet her, happy at last.

But Abanazar heard about Aladdin's riches and wanted the lamp more than ever. So he went to the palace, calling out: "New lamps for old!"

Princess Badra didn't know Aladdin's lamp was magic. When she heard Abanazar, she swapped his lamp for a new one.

The second he had the lamp, Abanazar summoned the genie.

WHOOSH!

"Take me, the palace and the princess far, far away NOW!"

The Sultan happened to look out of his window shortly after this, and screamed. Badra's palace had vanished.

He sent for Aladdin, who had been out hunting. "Where's my daughter?" he shouted.

"I don't know!" said Aladdin. "This is terrible. But I'll find her."

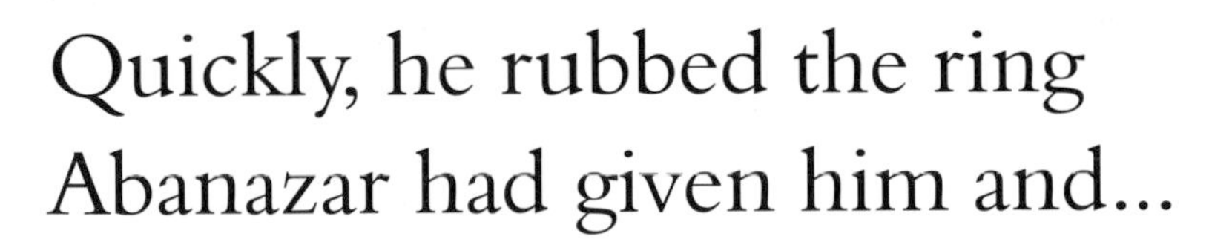

Quickly, he rubbed the ring
Abanazar had given him and...

PING!

...the first genie appeared.

"Please take me to Princess Badra – as fast as you can!" gasped Aladdin.

In moments, Aladdin was in the desert, at the foot of his palace.

"Abanazar kidnapped me," Badra called down to Aladdin. "So I poisoned his wine. But now I'm stuck here."

Aladdin thought of Badra tricking Abanazar and laughed. "Don't worry!" he shouted. "I've come to take you home."

With one last wish, Aladdin, Badra and their palace were whisked through the air and landed back safely, opposite the Sultan's palace.

In time, Aladdin became Sultan and had a son. Now, he was truly happy, so the ring and lamp were placed in a drawer. And there the genies sit, until they are needed again...

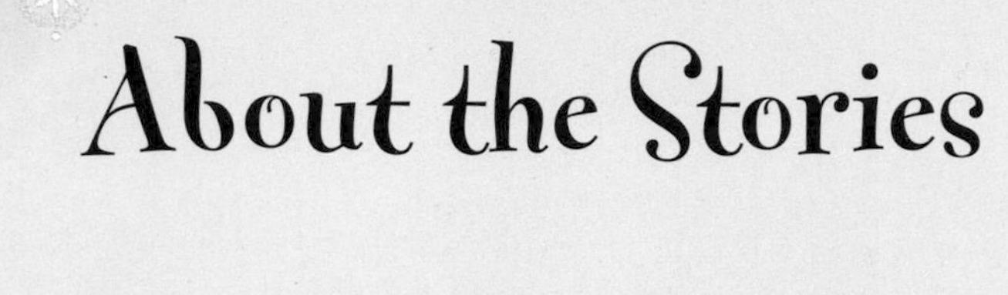

# About the Stories

## How Zebras Got Their Stripes

There are lots of different folk tales to explain why zebras have their black and white stripes. The story in this collection is based on an old folk tale from Namibia, in southern Africa.

## Brer Rabbit Down the Well

*Brer Rabbit Down the Well* is just one of many stories about Brer Rabbit, Brer Fox and other animal characters. They were written in the nineteenth century by an American named Joel Chandler Harris – but he didn't make them up completely. A lot of his stories are very similar to earlier African and Cherokee legends.

## The Dragon Painter

*The Dragon Painter* is a traditional Chinese story. People have been telling it for over a thousand years. Even today, people in China say "painting the dragon's eyes" to describe the finishing touches which bring a work of art to life.

## Why the Sea is Salty

*Why the Sea is Salty* is a traditional tale from Korea, which is where the tale in this book is set – but a similar story is also told in Sweden.

## Aladdin and his Magical Lamp

*Aladdin and his Magical Lamp* comes from a collection of Arabian stories known as *The Thousand and One Nights*. Aladdin's wicked uncle wasn't named in the first story – but he appeared as Abanazar in the first Aladdin pantomime, so that's the name he has in this retelling.

Designed by Louise Flutter
Digital manipulation: Nick Wakeford

First published in 2011 by Usborne Publishing Ltd.,
Usborne House, 83-85 Saffron Hill, London EC1N 8RT, England.
www.usborne.com 
UE. First published in America in 2012.